Festival of Frost

CHWilliams

Festival of Frost

C.H. Williams

ISBN- 13: 9781095401644

To the doubters

The Wilderness

Hidden Cove

The Dogteeth Hills

Quarry Lake

The Basin

Upper Great Fork

Witch's Wood

The Plains

Upper Miner Fork

Crooked Creek

Serpent Stream

Hilland's Dale

Merchant's Vein

Buyer's Bay

The Capital

Chapter 1

LILAH

"JULI!" LILAH'S SCREAM WAS LOST ON THE WIND, THOUGH, HER sister already too far gone to hear the cry.

The Basin, as the crevasse between the foothills was so aptly named, seemed happy to drink in the voices of the living.

Lilah frowned, watching her sister's silhouette disappear through the grass towards the bleeding sky.

Wasn't fair.

It wasn't fair that Lilah had been left stranded–not just in the field, though that was bad enough, having to wade through the sea of prickling stalks jutting this way and that into her legs as the sun sank, darkness already rising along the rim of the horizon.

No, it wasn't fair, being left so far from the world.

From her friends.

Her family, she thought resentfully, hadn't been so considerate. They'd trailed right along, determined to stick together.

Except now, when Juli, too, had at last abandoned her. There'd be stories around the fire, tonight, and Juli and Grayson reveled in the tales. It was, Lilah supposed, their only chance to leave this wretched place—and their reason—behind.

Still, Lilah refused to lose herself to the fantastical tales, and so the facts remained.

Her friends were too far away, left behind in the Capital. Her loony Aunt Bess was too close, now living in the room across the hall, a decrepit, half-blind old crone.

And Juli.

Juli, who'd promised to stay, but who instead went running off after boys and stories, leaving Lilah all alone in this gods-forsaken hell-hole.

Grabbing a fistful of grass, stripping the seeds from the chafe with an angry yank that left her fingers stinging, Lilah started off towards the house.

She didn't ask to be brought here.

She hadn't asked her father to rise before the Board of Commissioners and bid on the Basin.

She hadn't asked him to sell his life savings for this glorified ditch, shoved in the butt-crack of Aerdela.

And she sure as hell hadn't asked to spend those gods-forsaken weeks in a carriage, with Juli chittering on about what kind of boys would be in the Basin, only relenting when the summer heat reached a fever-pitch of near-suffocating degree.

Lilah had never been interested in romance.

Juli, as in all things, veered the opposite direction.

So much for sisters.

They didn't even look alike. Not anymore.

Fuck this place.

Lilah let the grass seeds trickle out of her fingertips, shoulders sinking in resignation as she walked.

Mother would accuse you of being spoiled.

Maybe she was.

Somehow, though, she didn't think so.

I'm not spoiled because I don't want to squat over a trench to take a pee.

But great leaders led by example, her father was fond of saying, and unless he wanted all the Basin twiddling their thumbs in an armchair, this had to be done with his family at the lead.

What he meant was that he couldn't afford to pay anyone to do this for him, because he'd pissed his money away just buying the damn land, and morality made a lovely blanket for their new-found poverty.

Night came quickly, in the Basin.

Not like in the Capital, where it pushed reluctantly into the space between the street-lamps, sidling into alleys after they'd all retired to their beds, waiting for permission to enter the city.

Here, it was a predator. It struck quickly. Without warning.

Merciless.

That, Lilah sort of liked.

It was admirable.

And anyway, the stars shown a little bit brighter in this corner of the world, so that was something, at least.

The grass hissed as she walked, following the game trail to the windows alight in the distance.

Her feet stopped her, though, as the lights grew closer.

There was nowhere to run, here.

Nowhere to go but the cabin.

To a bed she resentfully shared with Juli, who couldn't seem to just lay still, who tossed and turned 'til dawn. To a bowl of cold water and the mirror that laughably replaced a bathing room. To breakfast, eventually, of hotgrain, no butter or cream or sugar to spare her from the bitter aftertaste.

The air was cooling quickly, in the dark, still and quiet.

Yet, the grass hissed on.

The grass hissed, and an uneasy prickling rose on the back of Lilah's neck. Sweat still clung to her cotton shift, skin sticky with exertion, only the breeze of her now-stilled movements cooling the heat, and the grass hissed away in the undisturbed night.

She turned, eyes straining into the dark.

A pair of glowing eyes gazed back.

Chapter 2

JULI

JULI GLANCED OVER HER SHOULDER, WATCHING LILAH THROW HER hands up in dismay. Her sister's lips mouthed something—some sort of chastisement, probably, knowing Lilah—but it didn't matter.

She was too far gone.

And tonight was story night.

Juli had to run the last little bit, trying to make it back to the settlement before the sun set completely, and she was out of breath, pushing open the door of the cabin, sweat making her hair cling uncomfortably to her forehead, but again, it didn't matter.

She hadn't missed it.

Everyone was gathered before the fireplace in the great room, Grayson waving her over.

"Gods, you're a sight," he whispered, a smile twitching at the corners of his mouth as she wedged herself beside him on the sofa.

"Shut it, ferret-face, you're one to talk," Juli snarked back.

Maybe it was a new-found love of the Basin that prompted Grayson to abandon the ridiculous finery of high-collar tunics and suit-tails and lacey sleeves he'd flaunted at the fetes in the city.

More likely, though, it was Nik.

Grayson would've probably stripped to his undershirt, if Nik asked.

Her brother settled, though, for easy cotton tunics with canvas pants.

"Where's your boyfriend," Juli demanded under her breath, eyes searching the room for the black-haired beauty her brother worshipped. As if she could stand another night being the buffer between longing glances and awkward would-be flirtations. Not after the fight with Lilah in the field.

It was an argument they had a thousand times, but the heat and the hunger and the sheer desperation of what their father had done, bringing them here, had at last bested the sisters.

It's your fault, Lilah had screamed. *Your fault Mama died!*

At least I was there, Li! Juli had yelled back tearfully. *Like always! I'm always the one that stays and takes care of things! The rest of you just—just run off, and I'm left fixing everything!*

Good riddance, leaving that girl in the field.

And if she could stave off playing intermediary between her brother and Nik, she *might* actually manage to enjoy tonight.

"Where *is* he," Grayson muttered, quite apparently worried. His pale blue eyes betrayed his thoughts, now, more than ever.

Not that there was much to worry about.

It was the Basin.

It wasn't like they had a surplus of boys, here, competing for Nik's attention, and anyway, everyone but Grayson seemed to be able to see Nik's infatuation with him.

But they'd keep on, in their ridiculous game of back-and-forth, leaving Grayson exasperated and anxious, Nik, angry and avoidant.

Not like her and Fin.

Gods, Finley was...

Well, Finley was fun.

Juli was watching Fin, now, as he scooted around the edge of the room, coming to sit cross-legged on the patch of floor in front of her. He leaned back, let her legs straddle his sides as he gave her a playful half-smile over his shoulder before turning to where Bess was shuffling to the armchair.

Grayson tensed, watching the two of them.

His anxiety was well-practiced, turning him of late from the angsty adolescent he'd been in the Capital into a thoroughly uptight young man with vastly too many inhibitions.

"You know what," Juli whispered, leaning over to Grayson.

His jaw clenched. "What."

And she could see it in his eyes, that he knew what she was going to say.

"You need to work this out," Juli breathed, straining to keep herself even. One argument was enough for the night, thank you very much. "You are killing yourself over that boy—"

"Don't you think I know that? Don't you think I am *living* that every gods-damned—"

"The two of you just need to fuck," she bit back, patience snapping. "That's all it is. Stop being such a prude. Go have a roll in the hay, and everyone'll feel better."

Grayson's face heated bright red, his knee starting to bounce violently against hers.

The living room was packed to overflowing, now, but there'd be others, crammed into the hallways, stretched out in the grass beyond the open window, trying to listen. Really, they should've moved this somewhere else, but their father was a stickler for tradition, and this was the first house that'd been built in the Basin.

Nearly a hundred, now, and there were more coming to the Basin every week.

The problem was, they weren't the merchants that ought to have followed.

They were the hopeless.

The destitute.

Anyone, thinking food might flow a little easier here, and hope, too.

They were wrong.

Winter was fast approaching, and their father had desperately written to the Capital for supplies—supplies that had yet to be requisitioned to him.

No money didn't buy a whole hell of a lot.

Juli had a plan, though.

Whispers of frost and doom, and she had a plan.

Her and Fin.

There were stories. More than stories. Strange people, living in the foothills. Game trails that curled east, too, towards an azure city by the sea. If he could stop brooding, she wouldn't mind if Grayson went, too, because really, he wasn't bad with a bow and arrow, and in the end, that meant they'd be no worse off than if they sat on their hands all winter, waiting for something to happen.

Waiting to freeze to death.

At least in the wild, they wouldn't have to hear their father bemoan the injustice of his spendthrift habits.

By all rights, she probably should've wanted Lilah to come along, but Lilah would've just scoffed, and given her a lecture about pulling her head out of the clouds.

Lilah didn't understand.

She assumed that Juli, in her optimism, simply didn't see the hopelessness.

That wasn't true.

Juli saw it.

And she defied it.

They'd come so far, wanting to see the world, and see the world they would, foolish or not.

Chapter 3

GRAYSON

GRAYSON WAS FUMING, SHOVED IN AGAINST HIS SISTER.

How *dare* she.

Her dark eyes glittered with mischief as she ran her fingers through Fin's sandy hair, her skin warm against Fin's porcelain.

Of all three of them, she was a spitting image of their mother.

At least, Juli looked like the pictures.

Never would their mother have looked on Nik with such contempt.

That's a lie, Grayson thought bitterly. The thought made his heart hurt. *Juli's right. He's killing me, and Mom would've hated that.*

But with the onyx hair, shining in the firelight against her hopeful-twilight skin, her slender form, light and airy, he sometimes wondered if Juli wasn't a little bit of their mother's ghost.

Nothing like Lilah.

Lilah, their father's daughter, except that she'd over-corrected. Her springy curls, what could've been loose ringlets, if she'd tried, were just pulled back into a tight braid. It never stopped strands from flying away, though, brushing her prairie-tinged cheeks.

And then there was Grayson.

Grayson, with his stupid blue eyes. They were his grandmother's, and that, he guessed, he didn't really mind, but still, everyone liked to talk about them. How different they were. How beautiful.

He'd've traded with Juli any day.

Traded his swallowed resentment for her sharp words, too.

Gods, it probably felt good, letting them fly so free.

Bess was sinking into the armchair, grimacing at the effort, now, and the chattering across the great room fell silent as she did so.

They called her Great Aunt Bess.

He didn't know whose aunt she really was. She'd been a governess, when they'd been children in the Capital, and so probably, she was somebody's aunt. Maybe.

"Once," Bess began, "there was a flower garden."

Grayson hardly heard the words, though, watching Nik catch his eye from the front door. The son of a smith from the Capital, Nik's family had been searching for something better beyond the city, and so when they'd had the chance to join the bandwagon and trail after a merchant forging the future of Aerdela, they took it.

"Be back," Grayson murmured, pushing himself off the sofa to make for where Nik beckoned him over with a tilt of the head.

"Gray—"

He gave her a pointed look, shaking his head. *Leave it be, Jules.*

She pursed her lips, gaze reluctantly drifting back to Bess—Bess, whose craggled voice was now droning on about what, Grayson couldn't have said.

Nik was grinning as Grayson met him at the door, and wordlessly, he took Grayson's hand, leading him outside beyond the packed house.

"What..." But Grayson trailed off, Nik pressing a finger against his lips. He was sooted and glistening, his cotton tunic fixed with a sprig holly in a buttonhole, hugging tight to each and every carved muscle as he turned, pulling Grayson along behind, away from the house.

They had plans.

The Basin would be theirs, some day. Grayson was the eldest. He'd inherit this land, and Nik would be at his side.

They'd dreamed it a thousand times, beneath the stars.

How lovely it'd be, commanding what would be a real honest-to-goodness city. And if it wasn't, they'd make it one. The Commissioners would listen to Grayson. Their father was flailing, that much, he could see, but Grayson—he'd been watching, learning, and he'd make the Basin into something great.

Nik pushed open the barn door, hinges creaking in the silent night.

It felt wrong, though, to break the quiet music of the Basin with words.

And so, he let Nik lead him up the ladder, to the hay loft.

Let Nik fall into the hay with a quiet laugh, dragging Grayson down with him.

Let Nik unbutton his trousers, tugging them down in between hungry kisses.

Let Nik roll him over, hands sure as they drifted across Grayson's hot skin, sparking with anticipation.

Let Nik fuck him, in the loft, beneath the stars.

Afterwards, they'd simply laid there.

Tangled. Inseparable.

Not a word between them.

Maybe Juli had been right. There'd been so much back and forth between them, this—this bonded them. Sealed them together. Removed the questions of what it all really meant, the kisses, the drifting hands, the lingering glances.

"I'm going back to the Capital," Nik breathed softly, head against Grayson's.

Grayson sat up, sure he'd misheard, pure terror turning his stomach to gravel. "What?"

"Me and Dad. We're going back." He pushed himself up, too, giving a small shrug. "Sorry, Gray. Staying here is...it's complicated. A death sentence, maybe, if things keep on the way they're going."

Grayson's heart was in his throat, disbelief turning his body into jelly. "Why—no, that—but we..." He trailed off, gesturing between them. "We were supposed to be something. We were going to fix things, here—and I told you, I would never let you starve—"

Nik's fingers trailed Grayson's jaw in a soft stroke. "I know," he said softly. "And I'm sorry, Gray. I really am."

"I—I could come with you—"

"No," Nik breathed, sighing. "No, I don't think that would be wise. I love you. I really do. But we're already gambling, going back. I can't support another mouth to feed."

"You don't have to, that—that place is my home, I have connections—"

"You had connections, Gray."

Nik's words cut deep.

He wasn't wrong.

Their father had burned every bridge, on the way out, bankrupted every account, destroyed every lifeline on his march to the Basin.

There was nothing waiting back home.

"Nik." Grayson's eyes found his, watery.

"You'll be okay," Nik was saying, brushing himself off, moving for the ladder. "Really, Gray. And if you're ever back, look me up, we can, er..." He gave a half-laugh. "We can do this again, sometime."

Do this again sometime.

Grayson let himself dissolve as the barn door closed.

You could only do something for the first time once.

There was no doing this again.

When it was over, it was over.

Nik was gone.

And Grayson was alone.

Chapter 4

LILAH

THERE WERE EYES, GLOWING IN THE DARK, AND LILAH WAS ALONE.

Rockwolf.

There'd been one, picking off goats, until Grayson shot it through the leg with an arrow, making a yowling mess of the whole damn thing.

So much for the archery tutor.

So much for leading by example.

There was no Grayson now, though. No anyone.

Lilah stooped to the ground, fingers groping for something—anything—

Gotcha.

The stone was still warm in her hand as she rose, eyes fixed on the flashing irises bobbing towards her.

With a quick exhale, she hurled the stone towards the beast. "Go on, scram—"

"Ouch!"

Lilah's hand fell limply to her side.

Impossible.

"Truce, truce—I surrender," someone was snickering, sounding more amused than hurt. "No more rocks!"

"Who are you," Lilah snarled, taking a step back.

An orb appeared a moment later, pulsing in the palm of a young woman's hand.

She'd pulled the moon from the sky itself, this woman, burning it molten as she held it in her hand, and yet, it seemed the most ordinary thing.

Like anyone could pluck a gem from the velvet sky.

"My name's Reed," she grinned, eyes nevertheless flashing, tossing the ball of light up and down with a playful air. "Didn't mean to scare you. Thought you heard me coming."

Pointed ears, coming to slender tips beneath easy, brown hair.

Night-eyes of a beast.

Fingers, filed to points, devious as the sharp rows of pearly teeth forming that mischievous smile.

"You're supposed to be a legend," Lilah whispered, eying the mountain elf with cold derision. The time for magic had passed. It was fading, and the elves would do well to remember that. "What are you doing here?"

"I might ask you the same question, human," Reed mused, taking a step forward, ball of light still in hand. "You shouldn't have come here."

"This is *our* place—"

"It is not," Reed snapped. "It belongs not to you." Her smile had faltered into a snarl, teeth barred. "You would do well to leave," she hissed, "leave, before the Festival of Frost."

Lilah scoffed, turning on her heel.

In the Capital, whispers of the Wilderness were fading into the stuff of legend, but in the outer edges, where life was simply beginning, everyone knew better.

Here, magic had not yet learned that its place was in the annals of history and the long-dead memories of those who'd fought.

And the elves had not learned their disappearing trick with the fluency of their southern siblings.

"It is old magic," Reed warned, following behind, sending the grass hissing once more. "That's why I've come. Your father—"

Lilah spun around, anger sparking "You've spoken with my father?"

"He will not heed my warnings—"

"Warnings? Of berry-lovers and nut-gatherers? You descend from the mountains to stir trouble," Lilah bit back. "Go. Fade away. Your time is done, *vora*. Your era is over. They might believe in your superstitions, still, in the south, but that is all they are! Superstitions!" Her breath caught angry in her chest.

The *vora* were tricksters.

That much, she'd learned from Bess.

Mostly, they stayed in the rumors, hiding in whispers, but this one had been brave, venturing down from their mountain caves, descending to the foothills no doubt to terrorize the new arrivals.

That her father hadn't heeded the warning—perhaps it was the only thing he'd done right.

"It will come," Reed said quietly, backing away, "whether you believe it or not. The Festival of Frost is encroaching. It strikes, like a coppermouth snake, when you are not looking, without so much as a rattle. Run, Lilah. Run fast. Don't look back." And with that, the *vora* turned, departing in darkness.

Lilah was left standing alone in the field with the grass and the stars and her own disturbed thoughts.

Juli would take the *vora* at her word.

Grayson would laugh it off, but secretly, he'd be scared, and would probably follow Juli's lead.

Nobody would listen to the youngest sister. Nobody would listen to Lilah.

So she wouldn't tell them.

It was a trick, most likely. The *vora* did that, sometimes. Tricked humans. It was probably a trap, because there was nowhere to run, here, in this bowl of a Basin. The nearest settlement was weeks away, at best, and that, if they went on horseback. Between them and the settlements, though, lay miles and miles of Wilderness, full of what, Lilah did not care to imagine.

Rockwolves would be the least of their worries, though.

The Wilderness lay untamed. Unchecked.

Coppermouths and grass-skuttlers would be nothing. There were the Sleeping Stones, the ones that could swallow a person whole without them even knowing, and the Fire Lilies, oozing oil from their tender leaves, oil that could burn a person's skin clean off, if they weren't careful, and that didn't even account for what sort of foul creatures the *vora* had dredged up from gods knew where.

It was nonsense.

All of it, nonsense.

The Basin might be the butt-crack of Aerdela, but it was a hell of a lot better than what else was out there. At least here, there were known dangers. Cold. Starvation. Out there lay the same—and more.

Lilah found the house emptied, when she finally dragged herself up the cabin steps.

She'd missed story night.

Juli would talk her ear off as they lay in bed, no doubt, recounting all of Bess's tales, talking about Fin, and how cute Fin had looked tonight, and how sweet Fin was, and on and on and on, as if Lilah didn't have better things to do with her night than listen to Juli drone on about her petty little romance.

Like that was the only thing in her fucking world.

The bedroom was empty, though, the bed still made as Lilah struck a match, lighting the room.

Maybe Juli had decided to start holding grudges.

Not that she had any right to.

Not when it was her fault Mama was dead.

The fever had left their mother with ashen skin and charcoal lips and dead, so gods-damned dead. It was supposed to be a relic of their grandmother's time, but it'd found them, all the same, and what did Juli do but walk away with but her life.

It didn't matter what Juli said. In that girl's hands lay healing, and she'd had a choice, Juli did.

Lilah didn't bother to strip off the cotton shift before collapsing onto the bed, exhaustion in her bones.

Juli wasn't coming back tonight, so there'd be nobody to complain that she was gross and sweaty and smelled sort of like garlic gone bad. She'd rise early, take a dip in the river before the rest of the settlement awoke.

The thought sounded rather pleasant, actually.

Letting the chilled water take her.

It was with these thoughts that she let herself drift into uneasy sleep.

The cold chased her dreams, shooing away traces of the hot, late summer night. She dreamt she could feel the water, ice against her skin. That it could send goose-prickles all up and down her arms. That it burned her toes to freezing, that it turned her nose to ice.

When Lilah awoke, she was huddled beneath the blanket, curled tight into a ball.

Dawn was just now peering through the window.

The window, Lilah realized with a jolt, that was covered in a fractal pattern of white, crawling along the glass.

Her breath frosted on the air as she pulled the blanket tighter, panic starting to rise.

Dreaming. You're just dreaming.

The breakfast bell clanked down below, though, and still, her fingers felt numb with cold.

Outside, the chill had coated the grasslands, the barn, everything, blanketed in hoarfrost.

The Festival of Frost, Lilah thought, rising from her bed.

Impossible.

Chapter 5

JULI

A GLISTENING WHITE BLANKET COATED THE BASIN AS DAWN MET THE day.

Like someone had dusted sugar crystals across the settlement.

"It's odd," Juli murmured, thinking aloud. She gave Fin a side-long glance, pulling his jacket tight around her shoulders as they walked.

The neighbors were staring–though not at her, this time. No, this time, they didn't care that she walked proudly across the settlement in the dress she'd disappeared in last night, Fin's hand in hers.

Just as well.

It was none of their gods-damned business.

"That's the Basin, though, isn't it," Fin shrugged, glancing around. "I mean, goes from sun to rain in minutes–weather's more than liable to change overnight, Jules."

He wasn't wrong.

Juli eyed the droves starting to wind their way towards the house, looking for breakfast. The rest of the shelters could only laughably be called proper houses, really nothing more than something to keep the rain and wind off their backs. Smokestacks were left cold, Basinites opting to seek their comfort in the warmth of the Commissioner's house rather than light up their own stoves.

Their father had manufactured an astounding level of dependence in a relatively short amount of time.

But he loved to feel important.

He loved when the people turned to him, even if he had no answers.

He wouldn't love it so much, she mused, when they realized he could do little more than offer empty reassurances.

The wagons will be here soon.

I've written for supplies, and I know they're on the way.

Ah, the lies he told to stroke his ego.

"Well," Fin edged. "So much for leaving before the first frost." He gave her a side-long glance, brow creased in worry. "Jules, I dunno. I just–I have a bad feeling about taking off. If the weather's already shifting, we're not going to have much of a chance to get our feet on the ground, and then what? What if we can't hunt, or–or find another settlement?"

"Then don't come with." Her eyes flicked back to the dirt path.

There was no room in the world for cowards. No time for second guessing.

"What if you just didn't go?"

"What if," Juli countered, picking up her pace for the house, "you just minded your own gods-damned business?"

Fin gave a sigh of exasperation, having to jog a few steps to keep up with her. "Jules! Please! Maybe if you just explained why it is you wanted to go so badly? And you don't have to invent stories, just tell me, I'll understand–"

Anger was rising in her heart.

She wasn't inventing stories, but it made sense that Finley would go on accusing her of things like that.

People didn't believe, anymore.

They didn't have any proper reverence, for the things of this world.

That *vora* girl, Reed, had said as much, when she'd warned of the Festival of Frost.

I told your father, Reed had said. *But he didn't listen.*

That fool. Of course, he hadn't. He clung to his rationality like it would save him, in the end.

This *was* the Wilderness.

This wasn't the Capital, where balanced ledgers and clean-swept stoops meant you'd live to see another day.

There were rules, here, rules that had to be followed. Their father didn't see that, and Lilah wouldn't, either. They'd been made from the same mold, those two. Too stubborn to see outside their own navel, too gods-damned incompetent to clean out the fuzz therein.

But Juli knew.

Juli knew what had to be done.

Find for me, these things three.

First, the pebbles, white as snow, round and smooth and brought from below.

Second, the berries, yellow as day, sweet and juicy and out of the way.

Third, the leaves as green as spring, winter's bounty to me you'll bring.

And when you gather your sacrifice three, only then, they'll leave you be.

Juli had frowned, listening to the rhyme. *Who's they,* she asked.

But Reed had disappeared.

No matter. Juli took no chances.

And it wasn't like there was anything better to do around here, not anymore. Not when Fin wouldn't take her seriously.

Writing her off, as if she was making up fairy tales—as if she had no right to believe. As if she, on principle, had no right to that world.

And, she thought, stomping up the steps of the cabin, yanking her hand away from Fin as he tried to grab it, if he wanted to stay here and die, that was his prerogative.

But she didn't have to.

Chapter 6

GRAYSON

DAWN CRAWLED THROUGH THE SLATS OF THE BARN, ROUSING Grayson where he'd drifted off in the hay.

Shivering as he unburied himself from the horse-blanket-and-hay bed he'd made for himself, he found his thoughts drifting back to what he'd done the night before.

Lilah always teased him for being soft. Or, she had, before she'd ensconced herself in that hardened, impossible shell of dislike.

But maybe she'd been right.

Maybe he'd fallen too hard for a boy that didn't really care.

His first time was supposed to be better. Last longer, too, he thought resentfully. Hurt less. There was supposed to be other things, oil, and the like, but in the moment, it hadn't mattered, because he'd just wanted Nik, and wanting was supposed to be enough.

It hadn't been.

The only solace, in Nik's leaving was that...well, that he was leaving. At least Grayson wouldn't have to see his stupid face again, avoid him awkwardly over breakfast, try and dodge him on story night.

The thought wasn't as sweet as he wanted it to be.

Hardly a consolation.

Nik took what he wanted. And he was gone.

It would be Grayson, like always, to pick up the pieces.

He'd done the same, when their mother had died. Grieving and torn apart, he felt like he'd been fucked badly, then, too. His father retreated. The ledgers went to hell. And who had been left, but Grayson and his sisters.

At least Lilah and Juli had been there, that time, sort of.

Now, though, he was utterly alone.

But maybe he didn't have to be.

Sliding haphazardly down the ladder, he hit the barn floor, knees jarred with the impact, but it didn't matter. Lilah—her condescension would run wide. She'd want to know why a barn, of all gods-forsaken places, why Nik, of all gods-forsaken people. But in the end, she'd purse her lips, wrapping her arms around his waist all the same. His baby sister. Juli—Juli would laugh, incredulous, that he'd been so reckless, so hasty. She'd lecture him about the art of intimacy. That it couldn't be rushed, that she, with her one lover, knew everything about how these things worked. But her smile would falter, after a time, and she'd lean her head on his shoulder, sympathetic.

Things could be sweet, again.

Time didn't have to tear them all apart.

Grayson opened the door to the back of the barn.

And froze.

Stupid. Stupid boy.

He'd been fucking in the hay loft, and that *vora* had been right. She'd come to warn him, and she'd been right, and it had sort of worried him, but he wanted Nik more than he wanted to worry, and *she'd been right.*

The barnyard was a slaughterhouse.

Littered with feathers and blood, the chicken coop had been eviscerated, feet and half-eaten chicken heads scattered on the frozen earth. Bloody carcasses of now-felled sheep were left, gruesome markers across the hill behind the barn, evidence of a clash, and in the distance—

Grayson's heart almost stopped.

A single cow, lowing in fear.

A flash of blue, spindly fingers splitting the earth apart, a flurry of white, a flash of fangs, and the cow fell, dead.

The creature licked its bloody lips, spidery hands working to de-flesh the poor beast, licking the raw strips of meat clean before sucking them down. Drawn of icicles, limbs splintering out in fractals, it was a nightmare come to life.

Grayson didn't move. Didn't dare to breathe. Would've stopped his own heart from pounding in his chest, if he could.

No pebbles. No berries. No leaves.

Maybe it was superstition, but he'd have given anything, in that moment, for even a fighting chance.

The morning bell clattered across the settlement, and the creature's long, narrow head snapped to attention, bloodied fingers stroking the air in agitation.

And then it vanished, in a puff of fog.

Gone.

Gone, and Grayson was reeling.

The Festival of Frost.

It was real.

And it was here.

Chapter 7

LILAH

LILAH GLANCED UP, WATCHING AS GRAYSON SANK DOWN ON THE bench beside her before an almost-cold bowl of hotgrain. "You stink," she muttered, wrinkling her nose. The smell of horse and hay was strong, bits of each still clinging to his tunic.

He said nothing, though, eyes vacant as he pulled a glass of water towards him.

The kitchen had mostly emptied out, most everyone else gulping down their food, disappearing outside to watch the unmelting frost glisten in the morning sun.

As if watching it was going to do anything.

The Festival of Frost. Lilah had half a mind to ask Aunt Bess about it, because it seemed like the sort of thing that crazy old bat would know about, but to ask was to confess her own doubts, and she had no doubts, because it was a childish superstition, that was all, meant to scare little kids into going to bed early and eating all of their vegetables.

It's a coincidence.

A vora comes to warn you about the Festival of Frost, and the next morning, we're in a winter wonderland, but yeah, Li. It's probably a coincidence.

Juli was falling down across the table from them both, looking cross. "Fucking Fin," she muttered under her breath, not bothering to look up at either of them.

At last.

Sweet little Fin had finally disappointed her.

That was what people always did, and Juli would be better off learning that sooner rather than later.

"What happened with Fin," Lilah whispered under her breath, gloating.

"Him first," Juli snapped back, thrusting a spoon at Grayson. "You've got hay in your hair."

But Grayson's pale eyes were distant beneath a furrowed brow. His mouth fell open to speak, but nothing came out, and he just shook his head, eyes tearing up.

Oh, Gray–

A shout from outside broke the moment, though, and Lilah was on her feet, eyes wide.

Calm down.

It's nothing.

You're jumpy from a night of poor sleep, that's all.

CLANG

CLANG

CLANG

Three bells–trouble. Wolves in the barnyard, foxes in the coop, and it wasn't nothing, that much was apparent as she followed the shouts of panic out of the cabin and down towards the barn, her brother and sister at her heels.

"I–I was going to tell you," Grayson was half-whispering, having to run a little to keep up with her long strides. "Li, brace yourself..."

A massacre.

There had been a massacre behind the barn.

Winter provisions–they'd needed that livestock, if they had any hope of making it through the winter months, and now...

Grains would only get them so far. Forget the milk, eggs–that'd been enough to see them through to spring, at least, when they could send more wagons south for provisions.

Someone was speculating loudly, voice carrying across the settlement, drawing out the rest of the people from their morning duties. "Had to have been one of them rockwolves–they've been creepin' around..."

"That wasn't a rockwolf," Grayson whispered, giving Lilah's sleeve a sharp tug to get her attention.

Juli frowned. "Li, there was a *vora* nosing around the settlement–"

"I saw her, too," Grayson nodded. "Reed, right? Talking about the Festival of Frost?"

Lilah frowned, jerking her arm back from her brother's grip. "Get a hold of yourselves. This isn't..." What it wasn't, though, she didn't know.

A few people were trying to scavenge what little meat remained from the carcasses. A woman was crying as she watched from the split-rail fence.

Juli was right. It couldn't be a rockwolf.

Even a pack wouldn't have demolished an entire settlement's worth of livestock, not with such silent ease.

"I saw it," Grayson was saying softly, now, pulling both of his sisters out of earshot of the congregation.

"You...saw what did this?" Juli asked, watching him. "Gray, why didn't you say something?"

"It–I–*you* wouldn't have believed it," Grayson snapped back.

He wasn't wrong.

Too much romance in that boy's head, and a bit too much whiskey of late, too, and Lilah half-wondered if *she'd* been at the drink, looking at the carnage around them.

It scared her.

"It doesn't matter, though," Grayson was saying, dropping his shoulders in resignation. "The *vora* was right. There's something wrong with this place. We have to get out of here."

Lilah sucked her teeth, watching her brother. Grayson, as a rule, wasn't overly fond of decisiveness. He mostly took Juli's cue, followed her lead. He was comfortable on the side-lines.

"So, what, if she was right? What if this is the–the Festival of Frost beginning? How are we possibly going to be safer somewhere else," Lilah asked, trying to keep the chill from her voice.

"I don't think that was what Reed was trying to say," Juli countered. "The bit about the berries and stones and such? That sounded like a ward to me."

"Berries?"

"Three things," Grayson echoed, nodding. "Pebbles, berries, and leaves. Jules is right, it sounded like the wards Bess talks about in her stories."

"Wards and–and monsters?" Lilah scoffed. "Listen to yourselves. These are children's stories!"

"You know what, Li?" Juli had her hands on her hips, glaring. "I'm getting kind of tired of this condescension–"

"It's called being reasonable–"

"It's going to be called 'being dead,' if we don't do something,"

Grayson muttered, voice low. His pale eyes flicked between them, uncertain.

Lilah's breath was catching angry in her throat, heat rising.

But there were no words, because he was right.

Grayson was right.

"What is father going to do," he pressed, glancing between them. "Write to the Capital again? At the very least, we can make it to another settlement, ask someone else to help us get supplies. That's reasonable, isn't it? Get someone to talk to the Capital on our behalf? And Jules and I can find the wards on the way. You don't have to help. Hell, Li, you don't even have to come. But I can at least make sure we've got food, yeah? I can hunt? And you're unbeatable with flint and steel. But what do we have, keeping us here for the winter? Food? Father's excuses? I'd rather die trying to do something than waiting for someone to save us."

Chapter 8

JULI

JULI'S PACK WAS DUMPED CARELESSLY AT HER FEET, STUFFED TO overflowing with bread and hard cheese. She'd wear what clothes she wanted, and had looped what she needed into a sort of bed-roll. With the weather shifting colder as the day wore on, she wouldn't have to worry about suffocating beneath her thick winter cloak.

Quite the opposite, in fact.

Lilah, on the other hand, looked unwilling to let go of summer. She only snipped, though, when Juli had said something about it.

"I tried to talk to Father," Grayson sighed, coming around the side of the house, his own bag slung across one shoulder, bow and quiver over the other. Stubble roughed his cheeks, tired circles beneath his eyes.

"And," Juli prodded.

"Er, 'tried' would be the operative word, Jules. Everyone wants his ear." Grayson shrugged. "I left him a note. He's not going to miss us."

That much was true. Even before their mother had passed, their father had a knack for disregarding his children for the sake of soothing his own sense of importance. Truthfully, Juli couldn't recall the last time she'd even seen him, walking about the settlement—or maybe she couldn't recall the last time he'd seen her walking about.

She saw him all the time.

At dinner, talking up whoever had complained the loudest that day.

On story nights, sidling up to Bess.

In the mornings, giving hearty claps on the backs of farmers tired of his lollygagging.

He never saw her, though.

"What's the plan," Juli asked, heaving her pack up.

Grayson nodded towards the foothills. "North."

"North?" Lilah's screech of outrage stirred the flock of ravens cawing in a nearby tree. "North, Gray? Why? There's no settlements that direction!"

Lilah was here resentfully.

Here, because of terror she didn't want, because of bloodshed she hadn't wished to see, and here, because through the fear and the worry, she knew as much as Juli and Grayson that blood and frost would not be all that drenched the Basin floor, for if they had been hopeless before, Juli couldn't say what it was they'd be, now.

"There are settlements," Grayson corrected. "Just not human ones. That's where the *vora* came from."

"We can get some answers," Juli cut in.

"Exactly." With a small shrug, Grayson looked each of his sisters over in turn. "Let's go, while there's still daylight left."

Juli's eyes lingered on their brother, though, and she made no motion to move. "What about Nik," she asked quietly. It was less of a question and more of a confirmation, because she saw plain enough.

Grayson, who had the night before been a mess, his heart tangled with the thought of Nik. Grayson, who'd disappeared with Nik, and Grayson, who'd showed up the next morning a mess, and though he tried to hide it beneath whatever fear the beast in the barnyard had sparked, he was hurting in a way that had little to do with the cold reality of the winter ahead.

"Nik's leaving," Grayson breathed. It was like the words gutted him. "Told me last night. He's going back to the Capital with his father. Thought it wasn't worth staying here." He glanced over Juli's shoulder, eying the movement as the others tried to drag the corpses from the field, already a pyre going in the south lot. "He's right, though," Grayson sighed, turning for the mountains. "There's no point in lingering."

It wasn't hard, sneaking out of the settlement, nor could it truly be called sneaking, by any reasonable definition of the word.

Really, they just wound around the back of the house and followed the game trail through what might, if they all survived to see the spring, become fields someday.

Only when they'd left the earshot of the settlement, with all the hemming and hawing, and the silence had settled over them all, did Juli realize it'd been a long time since they'd been together. Just the three of them. Alone.

It'd last been the funeral, now that she thought about it.

Two years ago.

They'd all gathered to sink their mother into the ground, and afterwards, Lilah had locked herself in her room. Grayson had gotten drunk at the wake, and Juli...Juli had just sat there, by the grave, waiting.

Not ready to say goodbye.

"I miss Mom," Juli said softly, breaking the quiet.

Grayson glanced over his shoulder, brows knit, as they always seemed to be. "Me too," he nodded quietly.

Only Lilah said nothing.

Just glared at the ground, blinking back tears.

She'd been too young for death.

They all had, clearly, but Li especially. Fourteen when their mother had died, and Lilah had a difficult relationship with her, anyway. She and Grayson, they threw to their father's side of things, something they both seemed to sort of resent, with their fawny skin and taupe-and-umber hair. Only Juli bore any passing to the woman she'd called mom.

From the Coastal Reaches, she was beautiful.

Not beautiful, the way the women in the Capital tried to be, beneath their whale-bone corsets and frumpy frocks.

Eva didn't ever have to try.

She woke up beautiful. She met the day beautiful. She faced council meetings beautiful, balanced the ledgers beautiful, and she'd died beautiful, too.

Two years between each of the kids, and that'd left Grayson of age, when she'd passed. He was poised, too, to take over the family, until their father had rallied and bought the Basin.

Some sort of rallying.

More like failing on an epic scale never before seen by humankind.

But they would do this.

They would find help for the settlement. Find the ward, prevent another massacre.

And they'd do it together, like their mother would've wanted.

Chapter 9

GRAYSON

JULI HAD THRUST THEIR MOTHER BACK INTO GRAYSON'S THOUGHTS. He watched Jules, feeding the fire in their feeble camp, Lilah brooding, huddled beneath her cloak.

What would Mom say now. Father, off the deep end. And me, dragging her daughters through the wilderness.

His sisters.

For all Li protested, she'd come along all the same. Maybe she didn't want to be left alone, waiting for their father to eventually notice his children had vanished. Or perhaps the morning massacre had been enough to convince her that staying in the settlement wasn't a guarantee of safety.

If anything, it was proof they couldn't stay.

The creature had spent most of the day lurking in the back of his mind, pushed aside by his tumbling thoughts about where to make camp and whether they should keep to the game trails or follow the setting sun, but as darkness encroached, the spindly beast came crawling forward one more.

He'd described it to his sisters as a monster.

They did not need more.

Juli had met his eyes, then, as he told them what he'd seen, coming out of the barn, and it seemed like she knew he couldn't have summoned the words to describe it in all its terrible splendor, anyway, even if he'd wanted to, which he didn't.

He wondered, picking at a piece of bread, if Nik and his father had left yet. They didn't have much to pack up. They could've been gone in ten minutes, if they wanted.

No horses—not if they'd left today—and it'd be a month on foot to the nearest settlement towards the south. They might be able to bum a ride from someone, or else trade some work for a couple of horses, maybe, but more likely they'd try and start something else. More than likely, they'd never quite make it back to the Capital.

It'd been stupid.

This idea, the one he'd toyed with, where he saved himself for Nik. Where his whole life of failed relationships and pitiful flirtations had been for a reason, and that reason was the blacksmith's son.

"So," Juli said, voice hollow. The fire was roaring, now, the heat a pleasant armament against the chill that was settling down around them. "The wards."

Lilah scoffed, pulling her cloak tighter. "I still think we need to find another settlement. Why should we take the word of the *vora*? If they knew this—this Festival was coming, why didn't they tell everyone? Why only warn us?"

"If the ward is as simple as some rocks and berries, maybe they thought they didn't have to," Juli shrugged.

"Rocks and—ugh!" Lilah rolled her eyes. "It's not like all that was just rolling around in a kitchen drawer! She didn't even tell us where to find any of it—"

"She did, though," Juli countered, glaring. "*First, the pebbles, white as snow, round and smooth and brought from below*—that's got to mean downstream, right? And the berries—*sweet and juicy and out of the way*—that means they're rare, hard to find. As for winter's bounty—not that much could be green, this time of year."

"That's my point exactly! 'Below' and 'out of the way' are such obscure instructions—they're meaningless! It's a clever rhyme..."

Lilah's voice trailed off, the girls continuing to bicker back and forth, and Grayson let his thoughts overtake him.

Nik was leaving.

Nik...was leaving.

"Maybe she didn't just tell us," Grayson said softly, and Lilah shot him an incredulous look. "No, listen. Nik's leaving. But he and I—we had plans, Li. We made promises. There's no way he'd just break his word, not unless there was something else going on. And there was something pinned to his shirt, this little cluster of berries and leaves, all tied in this bulky twine—I'd bet anything there were pebbles there, too, only I didn't look."

Juli's expression was one of pathetic sympathy. "Gray..."

"No, I—I know how this sounds," he said, and he could hear the pitiful hope as his voice cracked. "But Nik wouldn't just leave! I'd bet anything that Reed talked to him, too. If we could find him, figure out where he got the wards from—"

"So, we go...south," Lilah frowned. "We've wasted an entire day on your half-cocked plan to find the *vora*, and now you've changed your mind?"

He ignored the remark, though, glancing to Juli. "What about Fin?

Something happened with you two. Did he say anything about leaving?"

She shook her head. "He accused me of making up stories. We..." Her shoulders sank, her golden eyes locking onto his. "We were planning on leaving anyway, him and me. He asked me to tell him the real reason. Didn't believe what I'd said about Reed."

"That doesn't mean she didn't talk to him," Grayson countered, glancing to Lilah. "Li talked to the *vora,* too–it's not a requisite for believing."

For whatever reason, Lilah's glare seemed to soften at the remark, eyes drifting from angry study of her brother to the ground at her feet.

"The question remains. Do we go look for Nik, and see if he's willing to give up how he got the ward? Or do we keep going north?" Juli asked.

It wasn't even really a question.

"We're not that far from the settlement, still. If we circle back, we can still catch him and his father before they're too far gone."

"Or we can find the wards ourselves." Lilah was watching him with fire in her eyes.

Juli's head snapped over to her sister. "What?"

"What kind of lover believes destruction is coming, and leaves you behind," Li said softly, not breaking Grayson's stare. "Jules didn't. Doesn't matter how foolish it is, believing this nonsense. You don't leave people you love behind like that. I know you're hurting, Gray. I know you want to believe there was a reason for why he left. And there is. He's a jackass. We should go north. Trying to find the *vora,* track down the wards..." She shook her head. "I think it's bullshit. But it's more reasonable than believing Nik did what he did out of necessity. It's more sane than thinking he had a good reason for hurting you."

Chapter 10

LILAH

CURLED UP BENEATH HER CLOAK, LILAH LISTENED TO THE RISE AND fall of Grayson's steady breathing.

He wasn't asleep.

Nor was Juli, her arm tucked around Lilah's waist, drawing her in close.

The fire was burning bright in the pre-dawn twilight, none of them daring to let it go out. Grayson had risen, several times, stoking the embers and fanning it back to roaring, before returning to the make-shift bedroll where his sisters lay half-shivering in the winter air that seemed to have descended upon them.

You fool.

She could hardly believe the words had left her lips.

We should go north.

No. What they should have done was find a human settlement. Barter their labor in exchange for passage back to the Capital. Escape this gods-forsaken place once and for all.

The hills had been stained red with the blood of livestock.

Still, the sight of the gutted lamb, ripped to ribbons, vacant eyes full of fear...it was unstoppable every time she closed her eyes.

It didn't matter what had done such a thing, rockwolf or no.

Lilah didn't want to be anywhere near it.

She wanted, more than anything, to go home.

Wherever that was.

Lilah was lost in half-dreams of a non-descript house somewhere far away from *vora* and frost festivals when Grayson gave her a nudge.

She blinked back exhaustion, half on the edge of tumbling into unconsciousness as she lay wedged between her brother and sister. An admonition already half-off her tongue, she was moving to shove him right back, serve him right for waking her—

His finger was pressed to his lips, though, eyes wide as he nodded behind them.

A pair of eyes, glowing in the dark.

Vora.

Vora, if they were lucky.

Crouched down on one knee, he was groping for an arrow, bow shaking slightly in his hands.

Perfect.

That was just perfect.

Their only defense was a quivering twenty-year-old who could barely hit the target on a still summer day.

Lilah lay pressed against the cold earth, tucked in beside Juli, whose grip around her waist had tightened to almost-suffocation.

She could not tear her gaze from the glowing eyes.

Not just two, she realized, staring beyond the fire and into the dark.

Four.

Six.

Panic was rising as they bobbed through the night, the fire seeming to flinch and flutter to their movement.

Not *vora.*

Decidedly not *vora.*

Take the shot, Grayson! Come on, just shoot!

He nocked the arrow, drawing back–and he held.

You idiot, aim before you draw!

The arrow sputtered off, veering hard left from the eyes growing closer.

Something spindly seemed to be skittering towards them, darting back and forth like the sandcrabs of her childhood along the rim of firelight.

Grayson was fumbling with another arrow, now, beads of sweat on his brow.

A screech broke the night, chilling and long, and Lilah started with a sharp inhale, jolting to sitting.

There was no safety against the ground.

The ice that shattered the air had seemed to ignite something in her heart, a deep, burning kind of fear she hadn't known for a long time.

The kind she hadn't felt since their mother died.

Juli was trying to tug her back in close, like she always did when any of them were hurting, but Lilah yanked her arm away.

When Lilah burned, she needed space.

Lots and lots of space.

Juli had been furious that she'd locked herself in her room, after their mother died, because what Juli wanted more than anything was for them to grieve together. She loved that Grayson was heartbroken about Nik, because it meant she wasn't alone in whatever pain she was feeling, and that, Lilah realized, was probably why Juli wanted her to like boys so gods-damned much. So they could be disappointed together.

But if Juli didn't want to burn, too, she'd back off.

And in her heart, she knew it, because she let Lilah go without much of a fight.

"Li," Grayson warned, voice quaking.

She brushed him off, though.

They knew what she could do. And they knew there was no stopping her, once she'd made up her mind.

A thin, icicle leg, jutting with hoarfrost was testing the ground illuminated with the firelight, and then another, and another—

Great bulging blue eyes had been stuck at the apex of the legs, a mess of fractals hiding long, dripping fangs, and the thing hissed, charging them.

Lilah closed her eyes, and let the fire take her.

She was the flame.

The anger beneath the surface wasn't hard to find.

It'd been simmering for as long as she could remember. Juli's incessant chattering. Gray's indecision. Her father's own incompetence, the thoughtlessness, that her mother had just died without so much as an effort to go on living, the Basin, in all its hopelessness, the friends she had left behind, the enemies she'd carried with her, the boys she was supposed to love, the girls that never caught her eye—

The heat was beautiful, kissing her skin.

She heard, in the distance, a shriek. The crackling of skin, the roar of fire, the most delicious sound in the world, and someone tried to pull her away, Juli, probably, but she gave a scream of pain as her hand found Lilah's, burning.

Burning.

Burning.

Chapter 11

JULI

"LILAH!"

Tears were streaming down Juli's face, her hand blistering as she backed away from her sister. "Lilah, stop it! Right now!"

Perhaps the command had been enough.

More likely, though, Li hadn't heard it, and had simply decided to stop, from boredom or exhaustion, it was impossible to tell.

But the wall of fire that had roared up to the sky fell with a crash, and Lilah dropped her hands to her side, out of breath.

In the wake of the darkness, a crisped shell of the monster.

It was smaller in death.

A burned ball of legs and teeth, smoking viciously.

And this was the girl who did not believe.

Who did not fear, that was more likely, if this is what she could do.

Grayson had abandoned the bow in the dirt, and was pushing Juli's hair back, now, taking her hand in his. "Jules..."

"Lilah first!" Her voice was watery as she glanced back to her sister, still staring at the corpse. "She—she was burning, you—"

"I'm fine." Lilah's voice was cold as she turned to meet their gaze. Her eyes softened, though, falling to Juli's welted hand. "Oh, gods—Jules—"

Already, though, Grayson had let her hand fall to her side, was rifling through his pack.

Oh, thank the gods.

He'd had enough sense to bring some salve.

It wouldn't do much.

But it might be enough.

Disoriented, a deeper, throbbing sense of pain was starting to well beneath the burn, and Juli squeezed her eyes closed, fighting back the wave of nausea.

She wasn't prepared for that kind of pain.

Didn't know, in truth, if she could survive it.

She felt Grayson take her hand once more, and winced, a glob of something cool and oily getting smeared into the skin.

There was something more than that, though.

Something more than the mix of relief and agonizing pain of the ointment.

Another fire.

Deep.

Unescapable.

Like a thousand pins and needles, and she was trying to hold back the sobs, now, as he worked her hand over mercilessly. There was a tang of iron in her mouth as she bit her tongue, swallowing another cry of pain—

"Jules." His voice was soft as he cradled his arm around her.

In the echo of agony, it took a long moment for her to register that the pain had faded.

Blinking back tears, she opened her eyes.

Red.

Irritated, to be sure, inflamed, a blistering residue callused across her palm, her fingertips, and it was shining with the balm he'd rubbed into the skin.

"Gray," she breathed, starting to shake, "what did you do?"

He only shook his head, lips pursed.

And she knew.

He hadn't done a damn thing.

This was her.

All her.

She knew there was healing in her hands. It was why she kept them close, her brother and sister, when they let her.

She had the Touch.

Maybe she'd sensed his hurt, when he'd tried to rub the balm into her hands. You could sense these things, with the Touch. Broken hearts as much as broken bones.

Maybe she'd been trying to fix him.

Or maybe she'd finally been tired of hurting.

Of grieving.

Of watching everything crumble and die, of fighting this hopeful fight again and again, of trying to fix everything and everyone except herself.

"Juli." Lilah's hand was trembling, reaching for her sister's arm. She paused, though, hesitant. "Juli, I'm so sorry—"

What she wanted to do was pull Li into a hug.

To hold her close, and Gray, too.

Instead, she retched, losing her dinner in the scorched dirt.

Chapter 12

GRAYSON

GRAYSON SHOOK THE COLD FROM HIS BONES, PACING AROUND THE fire—a fire he wasn't brave enough to ask if Lilah was fanning.

The creature lay, a crumpled mess, opposite them.

"We should move it," Juli whispered, where she sat in Lilah's arms.

Grayson nudged the singed carcass with the toe of his boot, watching as the movement shook a rain of ash onto the pale dawn earth. "No. It's a warning." He glanced over to Li, her look of skeptical disdain for once absent, leaving her looking painfully young. "What we should do is leave. Get up into the foothills. There's better shelter up there, and *vora*, too. They've avoided these—whatever they are—"

"Ice spiders," Lilah said softly, eyes sparking.

"Fine." Grayson felt the corners of his mouth twitch upwards. "The *vora* have managed to steer clear of the ice spiders for this long. It's like we agreed. Either they can help us, or at least tell us how to find the wards. Personally, I favor the latter. It's only a matter of time before the settlement gets hit. And..." He met Lilah's gaze. "They don't have Li anymore, which means they're vulnerable."

No Lilah to defend them.

No Juli to heal them.

And no Grayson to tremble like the coward he was.

He'd known his sisters were special.

Anymore, though, their talents were useless. What good was Lilah's fire in the Capital, where the best she could do was burn it to the ground? It'd been kept close, a family secret. Too many good men and women had already died for the talents they couldn't master.

Juli's Touch was easier to overlook. More useful. Nobody said anything about it, but she'd been good at mending from the start.

Then there was Grayson.

Grayson, the little boy who'd liked to play in the dirt.

Grayson, the adolescent who'd romanced his days away with lace cuffs and fetes.

Grayson, who'd sworn to be a different sort of man in the Basin.

Grayson, who got fucked in a barn and left behind.

You will have your moment, he could recall their mother saying. *There is some magic in you, yet.*

Not that he believed it.

Nor would she, if she could see them now.

Grayson pulled Juli to standing, then Lilah, trying rather clumsily to brush them off as he did so.

They left the beast, burned to a crisp, before the dying embers.

A warning of what they'd do.

Of what Lilah was capable of.

An omen not to follow.

But the ice spiders did, anyway.

The days waned into weeks, and the ice spiders followed.

Into the foothills, around the twisting switchbacks trod by game and *vora* alike, chasing the three of them up, up, up, to find an early winter.

Each night felt the same.

Grayson hardly slept.

They were supposed to take turns, ostensibly, but he didn't want Li, or else Jules, to be alone. Not that he could do much.

But at least he was a wake to watch Lilah's fire wall them in.

During the days, they kept watch for any signs of life or ward. Any pebbles, as white as snow, or berries yellow, or leaves of brilliant green. Any *vora,* friendly or no.

Nothing.

And it started to seem like folly, this fool's errand.

Only the ice spiders, and the thought of Nik's berried pin, kept Grayson going.

The only proof any of it was real.

There were patterns, though, some method to their wandering. The spiders loved the water. The closer to the river they kept, the more the spiders converged–the further they drifted, the easier the nights became. It became a game, then, of winding towards water in the mornings, veering off in the afternoon, praying there wasn't a hidden spring, or else some sort of lake or pond to take them unawares.

When water wasn't the aim, they followed smoke, the only evidence they'd yet to see of the *vora.*

But if the *vora* were camping in the woods, they were clever, their tracks left hidden.

It was from necessity that Grayson's aim with the bow and arrow had started to improve.

Hunt, or die, that much, they'd started to see quite quickly.

And Lilah could do a hell of a roasted hare.

The problem, increasingly, was Juli.

She was sick, and getting sicker.

Li had rightfully suggested they make something closer to a permanent camp for a few days, let Jules recover.

It'd done little for their middle sister.

She hardly kept down her food, her body aching all the time, and Grayson felt a looming cloud of guilt, pushing her forward.

Juli didn't want to stop, though.

She didn't want the rest they offered. The three days they'd settled, far from the river, she'd been hellacious, only Lilah's temper cooling her heels somewhat.

So they carried on, Lilah fighting off the spiders, Juli, sick, and Grayson, praying that soon, they'd find the *vora*.

Chapter 13

LILAH

"What do you mean, late," Lilah hissed, glancing over her shoulder.

Grayson had disappeared into the woods to take a piss, leaving Lilah and Juli milling about beside his pack where it leaned against a great pine tree.

"I mean, *late,*" Juli whispered. Her honey eyes were watching Lilah, voice trying to maintain some semblance of calm.

"How late?"

Juli only sighed, eyes flitting into the forest for any sight of their brother. "Late enough."

"That doesn't mean anything. You've been sick. We—we haven't been eating, not that much, the stress—I mean, I hardly even..." Lilah trailed off, at a loss. Her own cycle had been light. Hardly worth noticing, even, barely worth the linen strips she'd torn off the shift now ripped to ribbons inside her pack.

"Li, that's what I'm trying to tell you. I haven't been properly ill.

Just...late."

Lilah's eyes flicked up to meet hers. "You're sure?"

She gave a small nod. "I'm sure."

"You have to tell Grayson."

Juli just scoffed, sinking down beside their brother's pack. "What for? So he can fuss and fret more than he already is? He's losing hope, Li, day by day, and I am, too. We've got those–things–on our trail, we're chasing the *vora* through the forest. You really think adding a baby to that's going to help?"

Lilah frowned, crossing her arms. "You can't be considering keeping it?" They could find the herb, surely, in all this wandering–it'd be a task, collecting it under Grayson's watchful eye, but doable. They'd have to make a camp, a proper camp, really let Juli rest as the tea worked through her body, and Grayson was going to have to down a proper deer, but...

Juli only shrugged.

"Oh, gods." Lilah was watching her sister, searching for some hint of a plan. "Gods, Jules–you were planning this?"

"Fin and I wanted a family," she said dully, not looking up. "I'm not saying the timing is exactly what I wanted. We had plans. And I know Fin's gone, but that doesn't mean I don't want a family anymore. It...just looks a little different, now."

Juli and Fin.

And suddenly, it wasn't just Juli talking about boys. It was Juli. Living her life. A woman. Making decisions. Trying to move on.

"Please don't tell Gray," Juli said softly. "Not yet. It's still early, I might–it might not even make it. And you know, Li, that loss would kill him. He'd think it's his fault."

"What do I think is my fault?" Grayson was coming around a bush, brushing off his hands.

"Nothing," Lilah sighed, pulling Jules up to standing.

"Nik," Juli filled in at her brother's look of protestation.

That shut him down quick.

Grayson's eyes clouded with pain as he scooped up his pack once more. "I've been thinking," he said, voice shifting from the jovial tones of that morning to something gruff, harsh, even. "We need to start climbing."

"The mountains?" Lilah scoffed. "Gray, that's ridiculous!" Already, the weather was miserable in the foothills, winter moving into full swing. To summit the mountains would be a death-wish.

"We don't have another choice—"

"We have every choice! Let's go west! There is no purpose, consigning ourselves to a snowy death!"

"Your brother is right." A thin, airy voice cut through the argument, and Lilah started, turning.

Reed.

"You must go up before you go back down," she snickered, coming to lean against a tree. "Then again, you've been wandering about the hills for the better part of two months, so I suppose you're really not the brightest bunch, are you?"

"Watch it," Lilah snarled.

Reed only shook her head in dismay. "I gave you the riddle. The answers, laid out plain."

First, the pebbles, white as snow, round and smooth and brought from below.

Second, the berries, yellow as day, sweet and juicy and out of the way.

Third, the leaves as green as spring, winter's bounty to me you'll bring.

And when you gather your sacrifice three, only then, they'll leave you be.

"Those weren't answers," Lilah snapped. "That was poetry–and bad poetry, at that! Any idiot can rhyme!"

"Li." Juli's hand was on her sister's arm, holding her back with a ginger touch. She remembered still her sister's burn, it seemed, did not wish to repeat what she'd found in a moment of panic and anger. "We've been trying to find you," Juli said softly, watching Reed.

Reed's smile faltered, straightening up. "And I, you. These hills–they're changeable. Liable to swallow up braver travelers than you."

"Help us," Grayson said softly. His eyes looked close to tears as he watched the *vora*. "Please."

"I am bound by vow," Reed whispered. "I cannot."

Lilah threw her hands in the air, furious. "Then why–"

"Hush," Reed murmured, taking a step forward. "I cannot help you. Already, you outrun an enemy that should've torn you apart. You flee between water and land, camping where they're weak. But the dark days are coming. Already, the sun is beginning to fade, and soon, there will be no rest. And so, I will tell you a story."

"This is hardly the time–"

"A story," Reed echoed. "Now, listen."

Chapter 14

JULI

"IT IS BELIEVED," REED SAID QUIETLY, "THAT ONCE, THERE WAS A storm. "So violent and so wretched was it that it tore the land away and turned the world upside down. Rocks rained from the sky, and air was beneath their feet. The gods had no choice, then, but to seek shelter on the mountain top. But there, they found solace unlike the peace they'd known below–" She coughed, though, words cut off.

"Go on," Juli whispered, watching Reed.

"They found solace–" She was cut off again, choking, shaking her head. "I can't," she wheezed, fingers on her chest.

Grayson was reaching for his waterskin, but it was no use.

Reed was clawing at her neck, now, lips turning blue. "I'm sorry. I tried, I..."

But whatever she was, they would not know.

The blue tinge seeped across her skin, swallowing her words, a sickening smoke beginning to curl out of her lips in the place of the answer she'd promised.

And in a gentle puff, she turned to ash.

"No!" Grayson's anguish echoed off the rocks, and Juli swore, turning away.

If Reed had vowed not to help them, if her words were bound by magic, then the story must've had the answers.

Bess would've known the story.

That much, Juli was sure of.

"Maybe," she said softly, glancing back between Grayson and Lilah, "we should go back to the Basin."

It wasn't such a crazy idea.

They had Lilah, and her fire, and the Basin had Bess, with her stories. They could go home. Figure out what they needed to fetch, unravel the mystery with a little bit of...comfort?

That was banking on a lot, though, and Grayson seemed to know it, watching her.

Banking on the Capital, answering their father's demand for food.

Banking on the fact they weren't already dead, all of them, at the hands of the ice spiders.

If they'd somehow made it, if they'd managed to ration the grains enough, to stretch the food to try and last through winter, it was unlikely they'd be terribly kind to the deserters.

But there was Fin.

He hadn't known, when she left.

Hadn't known she carried their child.

Hell. *She* hadn't known.

He couldn't very well turn her away then, could he?

In her heart, she knew the answer.

Finley hadn't believed her, when she'd told him why she wanted to leave.

It was unlikely he'd believe her, when she told him why she wanted to return.

"Go back to the Basin," Gray echoed, taking a step towards her. "Jules, why? You heard what Reed was trying to tell us—we at least have to keep making for the mountains. After her warning, we can hardly afford to turn back." There was guilt in his eyes as he said it.

Like he thought he was the one making her ill.

Like it was such a bad thing, that she was losing her breakfast.

It would pass, soon.

And then he'd see. Then he'd stop feeling so bad.

"She thinks Bess might know the rest of the story," Lilah said softly.

Grayson shook his head, sighing. "I know Bess's stories. Spent my life listening to them. That one's *vora*, through-and-through."

"Fine." Juli pushed her hair out of her face, trying to think. "Fine, so it was a stupid idea—"

"It wasn't—"

"Give it a rest, Gray," she snipped. "Rocks rained from the sky, pebbles from below..." Her eyes skirted the ground before drifting up to the peaks in the distance.

The mountains.

It felt like such an insane, impossible decision.

And what was the alternative.

To stay.

To watch Lilah, exhausting herself each night, fighting back the ice spiders? She was burning herself out.

The last couple nights had been bad, too. Lilah had just laid there, after the spiders burned, trembling, eyes glued to the fire, like to lose sight of it was to lose herself.

Not that Grayson had been much better.

He'd tried, at first, with the bow and arrow. Night after night.

Eventually, though, he'd given up.

Resigned himself to what he thought must've been his own uselessness.

Juli had tried to fight the hopelessness, in her own way.

Tried to imagine the future.

Maybe it'd be in the Basin, and maybe not. It wouldn't be alone, though, that much she knew. That was what made it so much less terrifying.

They'd face monsters and demons, they'd run and they'd fight, and they would do it together. Always together. That was their strength—the love they held for each other.

"So, we're really going there," Juli said softly, wrapping her arm around Grayson's waist, nodding to the mountains.

"Yeah," he breathed. "I don't think we have a choice."

"We always have a choice," Lilah shrugged, leaning her head against his shoulder.

Grayson said nothing as they stared at the mountains looming ahead.

If the alternative was an unending fight, a dying settlement...it didn't feel like much of a choice. Not really.

Chapter 15

GRAYSON

THE FUNNY THING ABOUT MOUNTAINS WAS THAT THEY LOOKED A LOT closer than they actually were.

Winter settled down around them, resentful and cold, clinging to the most bitter weather it seemed to muster.

Reed hadn't been wrong about the days growing dark, and it couldn't have been far past noon when the wind and the dark clouds circling above had forced the three of them to shelter, retreating into a mercifully empty crevasse.

Lilah had struck a small fire at the back of the cave, coaxing it from nothing more than moss with her fingertips.

Her skills as a fire-render had grown in the months of running, honed in an almost nightly battle—a battle that had at last begun to wane the last few nights, thank the gods.

"I rather like this," Juli murmured, leaning back against the wall of the cave, surveying their home for the night. "By far the nicest accommodations we've seen in a while."

Lilah cracked a smile at that one.

The fire had scorched the ice spiders—and whatever cynicism that bound her to displeasure. To be sure, Li was still quick to offer condescension. But anymore, it felt tempered in a sort of wisdom Grayson hadn't known.

Grayson ran his fingers through his beard, stretched out on the bedroll by the fire.

Jules wasn't wrong.

It was tempting to stay here, at least for a day or so. Rest. Recover.

It went in bouts like that. Fight, and fight hard for days, weeks, even. And then nothing. A few moments to recuperate.

"Be back," Lilah muttered, giving Juli's arm a squeeze before turning for the mouth of the cave.

She left her brother and sister in quiet, the fire flickering down slightly at its creator's departure.

Grayson pushed himself up, scooting over next to Juli. "I figure, another week, we're at the summit," he said, eyes on the flurries tearing at the sky beyond. "We wait out this storm, rest a bit, and then push to the top." He glanced back to Juli, looking her up and down. "You've been better, lately."

"Better," she echoed, nodding thoughtfully. Then, bringing her gaze back to him, she sighed. "Gray, I...I wasn't ill. Not properly."

"You—"

She cut him off, giving his hand a squeeze. "Shh."

"Jules, what—"

"Hush." A faint smile was on her lips, now, as she pulled his hand towards her, moving aside the cloak to rest it gently on her belly. Her bulging belly, he realized, hidden deftly beneath the layers in the cold.

"Juli," he breathed, eyes finding hers. "Why didn't you say

something?"

"Wanted to make sure," she shrugged.

Grayson's chest tightened as he pulled his hand away. "We..." *We what?*

"Hey." Her golden eyes found his, warning. "Don't you dare do that. I'm fine. Don't you dare start coddling me now, alright? Don't make me regret telling you."

There was nothing to do, then, but pull her into a hug. "You need anything, though, you tell me, Jules. Anything."

"That was always true, Gray."

"Yeah," he snickered, pulling back, "it–"

He was cut off, though, by something trembling far beneath the earth, the squealing of stone-on-stone piercing through the air.

The fire puffed out in a splintering crack of dust and stone, and he was on his feet, dragging Juli right behind him into the storm.

Whatever they had awoken from inside the cavern, though, cared not for the raging wind and howling snow.

Stumbling through the blinding onslaught, Grayson watched in horror as the cave collapsed.

And from the rubble, a beast.

Terrible.

A man of rock, rising from within its den, hungry as it arose from years of slumber.

A Sleeping Stone, like from Bess's stories.

Awakened at last.

"Juli, run!"

Grayson's voice on the air only drew the creature on, great bouldered limbs flexing as it stooped, gathering a fistful of rubble, and in a single smooth movement, hurled the debris to where they both stood.

"No!" It was futile, he knew. Covering her body with his. Throwing himself in front of her. Like it'd do anything, against the weight of stone crashing towards them.

Eyes squeezed shut, he braced himself for the impact.

To be crushed.

Decimated.

To die, beside his sister, bearing the weight of rubble and the loss of life as he left for the underworld.

The impact never came.

"Gray," Juli whispered, hand on his back.

He hardly dared to look.

But above them, the rain of rock had splintered, falling aside in pulverized flakes where he'd thrown his arms out to protect them both.

He'd moved the earth like it was nothing.

Like feathers in the wind.

The Sleeping Stone gave a roar, moving for another round.

Me.

That's me.

I'm doing this.

He felt that much. Felt his body straining, felt the cold of earth in his bones, the humming that was running beneath his feet, but more than anything, the unwavering truth.

In that moment, he was what stood between life and death.

Catching his breath, he took a step forward, summoning his focus.

He'd done this as a child.

Played with pebbles on the beach. Loved to run the sand through his fingers, to feel the dirt between his toes.

Grayson didn't give it a second thought, sliding his boots off, letting his feet stand bare upon the snow.

And the earth reveled, meeting its brother.

Now what?

Lilah talked about anger.

He couldn't find it, though. Nik–gods, he hadn't thought about that boy in a while, but even still, there was only heartache.

Before the heartache, though, there'd been love.

And gods, that was the kind of love he hadn't known before. Wild. All-consuming. It took his waking thoughts, his dreams, and all the space between, and that–that was a powerful thing.

He let his thoughts drift back to the barn, another lifetime ago.

How badly he'd loved.

How he'd wanted, more than anything else in this gods-forsaken world.

Lifting his hand to the sky, he exhaled.

His cry of defiance echoed off the mountain as he returned the volley towards the Sleeping Stone.

Rock rained back and forth, the giant screaming in agony as each onslaught was sent hurling back, chipping away at it, until at last, Grayson sent one last cascade down, shattering the creature in an ear-splitting crash.

An in its wake, pebbles.

Pebbles, as white as snow, raining from the sky.

Chapter 16

LILAH

THE WINTER WINDS SNAPPED AROUND HER AS LILAH LEFT THE SAFETY of the cave. It didn't bother her, though.

She had her fire.

But today, more than the fire, she had her grief, too.

Days like today were just like her mother. A storm. A raging, wretched storm, the kind that you half-wanted to end, half-wanted to stay.

The sadness waxed and waned.

It was easy to be angry at Juli, at the woman with healing in her hands, for letting their mother die while she went on living. It was far more difficult, though, to grieve the bitter moments Lilah had shared with her mom. Moments that could never be rewritten. Measured, finite moments of resentment and conflict.

Juli and Grayson were a picture of a different life. Their parents, but happier. Better.

So where did that leave her?

Lilah blew out a breath, eyes drifting to the alcove of pines she'd taken refuge in.

The wind was nipping at her skin, recoiling at the fire in her blood.

If it wasn't for the others, she wouldn't need the shelter of a cave. She wouldn't need shelter at all.

She could revel in the onslaught.

I am alright.

Lilah had to force herself to believe the words, standing there alone. Love and solitude could coexist. They would not condemn her for taking her moments.

Not anymore.

Not like they had, after their mother had died.

I am alright.

This was okay.

This was permission, to love them from a distance.

This didn't have to leave her at odds with her own heart, because it was alright, to love them and be furious that they could relive days Lilah never got.

And so, Lilah watched the forest, reveling in the winter as her skin burned away the cold.

Lilah burned the cold away, and once she'd done that, she started on the dead leaves, dried to crisps and once buried beneath the snow that buried all but her. Branches and grasses and bark and trees, they all started to succumb, and she laughed quietly, watching her flame.

It belonged to her, and her alone.

Great columns of fire, reaching to the sky, and the spitting and hissing of winter dying was a swell of music to her ears. It was a song of defiance, screaming back all the words she'd wanted to say before her mother died. A song of mourning, regretting that in the barrage, there hadn't been sweeter words, too, from either mother or daughter. A song of rebellion, because they were both sinners.

The only difference was that Lilah knew it.

But their mother had been too happy to play the saint.

A tremendous crash broke the sound of crackling sap, and the fire faltered out, quelched by the snow as Lilah's head snapped back to the encampment.

Lilah froze, straining to hear over the embers of the inferno.

Juli's shriek echoed through the woods, though, and Lilah was running, fighting off the onslaught of the storm to find them.

She'd left them. She'd selfishly left them, defenseless, and the worst part was that she didn't want to go back.

She wanted them to be fine, she wanted them safe, but she wasn't Juli, keeping them close. She'd never asked to be their protector.

The encampment was decimated.

Lilah stopped dead in her tracks, breathless, watching as a mountainous stone man rose once more from the place where the cave had been.

Lumbering and massive, the creature had been wrought from the earth itself, a great grotesquery of granite, and with a roar, it hurled a boulder through the air—and straight for Grayson and Juli.

Lilah screamed, fire in her fingers.

But what could the flame do against the rock.

Grayson thrust his hands forward, grunting as he absorbed the impact of a thousand boulders falling from the sky, and with a push, returned them to the stone man.

The resultant crash was shattering.

Grayson had a hand around Juli's waist, the other held to the sky, shielding them both from the rain of snow white pebbles that burst forth as the stone man exploded.

A smile had split across his lips as he pulled Juli tight, and Lilah felt an echo of a laugh dancing on her tongue.

They'd done it.

They'd found them.

Their pebbles.

Juli was pulling away, giving Grayson's hand an admonishing smack—she must've told him, Lilah thought, watching as the last bits of dirt and stone fell to the ground, the last bits of the stone giant.

Grayson's eyes flicked to Lilah.

He was laughing.

Laughing, as he sank to his knees, running the piles of pebbles through his hands. Juli had pressed her hand against her mouth, fighting back tears that came anyway, watching.

And Lilah.

Lilah was making for them both, sheer relief flooding her bones.

Relief that she was not alone, anymore. That their lives lay, now, not solely in her hands, but in the hands of each other. That, more than the love they could give each other, there was fight in their hearts, and the understanding that they would not fail each other.

Not again.

Chapter 17

JULI

"OH, GODS, GRAY," JULI SNICKERED, WEIGHING HIS PACK IN HER hands. "Got enough, don'tcha?"

Grayson merely shrugged, expression serious. "I won't risk running short. None of us knows what this ward requires, and I do not wish this to become an annual pilgrimage, as much fun as running from ice spiders and Sleeping Stones is." His eyes flicked up to hers, though, and there was something playful in the pale blue.

This was real.

A pack, making his shoulders strain, pockets stuffed with rocks, and this was real.

More than three children terrorized by the minions of the Festival of Frost, driven from their home by *vora* whispers and a bloody massacre.

This was real.

"I bet you anything the berries are at the top of that mountain," Juli mused, leaning against a boulder, surveying what would doubtless be a wretched assent.

At least she wasn't puking her guts out every five minutes.

So there was that.

Lilah looked worried, though, joining her sister.

"What's wrong?"

"Nothing," Lilah muttered, "it's just...I'm wondering who it was that the *vora* made the vow to. It doesn't seem likely they'd swear a sacred oath to a herd of ice spiders. And I keep wondering, if someone had enough sense to stop the *vora* from spreading the news of a ward powerful enough to stop something worse than an ice spider..."

"Then who's putting on the Festival of Frost," Grayson asked, voice dark.

"Exactly."

They all exchanged looks, saying nothing.

The words didn't need to be said on the heels of such a victory.

"We should go, then," Grayson nodded, sighing. "Storm's passed—I'll take that as a good omen. Can't be a coincidence, we find the stones, and the snow stops."

A good omen—or a trap.

Juli wasn't prone to cynicism, but she favored the latter.

Perhaps so much time together, and Lilah had started to rub off on her.

The trek would've been slow going, if it hadn't been for their youngest sister, though. Burning bright, the snow hissed into great pillars of steam as Lilah led the way up the mountain slopes.

Grayson seemed lost in thought as he walked, a smile flickering across his lips every now and then, and Juli had swallowed a laugh when he'd sent little waves of dirt and stone into easy steps before them, saving her the bother of clamoring up the mountain side.

Juli had let her hand drift to her abdomen, the faint bulge feeling more familiar beneath her hand with each passing day.

It was hardly anything, yet. Like she'd been back in the Capital and eaten one too many pastries.

How could any of them go back, after this.

Return to fetes and lace after seeing the Wilderness. Seeing the magic.

The world was alive, and it was begging them to stay and play.

I promise, Juli thought. *I promise, my child, I will show you this world. The rest will forget the magic, in the end.*

But we won't.

We won't.

They would find the wards.

And they would rebuild the Basin.

Rebuild it proper, not the way their father had, haphazard and reckless, but thoughtfully, lovingly.

Only a few summer months in the Basin, and ice spiders had come crawling.

But when the danger had ebbed, what beauty would come forth in its wake? When they'd built their homes, when they pushed back the storms, when they'd armored themselves with the loving protection only brought by the fierce loyalty of brother and sister, what goodness could bloom, when given the chance?

A tremendous roar shattered through the air.

What goodness, indeed.

Towering above them all, with a snarl to shake the ground and fangs like the mountains they dared to summit, a great white bear.

It'd come from nowhere, caught on a trail where it'd been in solitude.

Lilah had thrown her fire into the familiar wall that guarded them in the night, but it was useless against the great beast.

Roaring up onto its hind legs, the massive bear let out a yowl as it crashed through the flames, white fur smoking as it caught, Lilah pushing the fire into its flesh.

Such pain, Juli realized.

Such agony.

Trapped.

"Stop!"

"It's a beast from the Festival of Frost," Grayson shouted back, arms straining as he sent the dirt around them swirling. His eyes were locked on a boulder easily as big as the bear itself, determination in his gaze.

"No, Gray–"

With a grunt, though, he sent the boulder upward in the air, hands raised to the heavens.

"They know!" Lilah snapped at her sister, pressing the flames in tighter. "They know, Jules! We're close–"

Juli had braced herself for the burning even before she'd thrown Lilah to the ground. Li had grown hotter, in their months of warring, and Juli felt her flesh writhing even as it mended itself, furious at the burning.

"Juli, back," Grayson warned, eyes locking on hers, the boulder wavering in the air above both her and the bear.

He couldn't hear it.

Couldn't hear the shrieks.

The crying.

All he saw, she realized, was a beast, rearing its head and roaring violence.

Of course, that was all he'd see. That was all he'd ever seen. Danger, around every corner, because that was what happened when he'd let go, once upon a time.

And Lilah...she remained the skeptic. Mistrustful of any and all.

Juli's body stood poised before the great white bear, eyes fixed unblinking on her brother. Her sister.

If it'd wanted to hurt her—hurt them—it would've, this, she felt in her gut.

For who would not go roaring through the trees when they saw a chance for reprieve.

Maybe it'd wished for death, at their hands. Fire and stone offered no mercy, though.

"Juli, move," Grayson growled, taking a step towards her, arms shaking with the strain.

"You've grown too used to fighting," she breathed, shaking her head. "You can't see anything but enemies, anymore. And it's true, they're all around. But I will not let you destroy what you don't understand just because you're afraid. You, of all people, Gray, should know better. And you, Li."

"Jules—"

"If you are so determined to end this creature, then end me, too," she said softly.

Arms wavering, his shoulders sank. And with a sigh, he cast the boulder aside, sending a rumbling crash through the trees.

The sound of defeat.

Juli turned to the bear, finding its glistening, black eyes.

So much pain.

And she had the Touch. She mended, hearts and hurts, all the same.

Gently, she reached out, fingers combing through the singed white fur, and closing her eyes, she began to work, humming as she healed.

Chapter 18

GRAYSON

MUSCLES BURNING FROM THE STRAIN, GRAYSON STOOD PANTING, aghast.

She was insane.

Juli was literally insane.

She'd thrown herself in front of that beast, like it was a wounded puppy, sat now, soothing it, her touch mending the burns and scrapes, remaking the creature.

Lilah was furious, fire sparking in her hands, but she did nothing except pace angrily back and forth.

To set the beast alight was to let the flames swallow their sister, too.

Juli moved with ease, fresh white fur left in the wake of the blackened crisp, and yet, even when the creature was whole, she kept working.

"Jules," Grayson muttered. "C'mon. It–it..."

But he trailed off.

What it was, exactly, he realized he didn't know.

Beneath her fingers, the fur began to shed, falling away in great, white clumps to meet the muddy ground where Li had melted the snow.

The bear only gave a soft groan, rolling over to expose its belly to her hands.

It'd been taller, too, Grayson realized with a jolt.

Hadn't it?

It had to have been.

Easily the size of the boulder he'd discarded, and now...

"Gray," Lilah whispered, her hand tugging on his sleeve. Her fingers were still hot, burning holes in the tunic, but he didn't care.

His eyes were fixed on Juli.

Juli, and the man now laying in the mud beside her.

She was whispering to him, now, this man with white hair, dark eyes searching her face.

"Li, get some water," Grayson mumbled, dropping his pack, sliding off his cloak.

Lilah stopped him, though, sliding her cloak off instead, leaving her in thin trousers and a tunic, ripped half-off by an ice-spider. "I'll be fine," she said softly, fire in her eyes. "Really."

He nodded dimly, taking Lilah's cloak as he edged towards Juli and the strange man.

It might be a trap.

An illusion, to prey on their sister's kindness.

But the man seemed half-conscious, slurred words dribbling from his mouth as Juli took his hand in hers.

"Here," Grayson muttered, tossing Li's cloak across the naked man.

Her eyes flicked to his, silent thanks written in them.

Don't thank me yet, Jules. He's liable to devour us still.

"What happened," Grayson nudged.

Juli only pursed her lips. "I don't know. All I saw was a heart that was hurting."

So was the Touch.

Mending heart and hand, all the same.

There'd been little choice, after that, to make camp.

Lilah struck the fire inside the shelter of stone Grayson had tumbled into being. The moving of the earth came back to him quickly, like something he hadn't even really forgotten. All the same, though, he wished it'd felt better, sending the rocks piling together.

Wished it'd been some sort of release for the anger he felt, at himself and at Juli.

He hadn't trusted her.

He believed that she'd been compromised, throwing herself in front of that monstrosity.

It'd been a foolish sort of thing she'd done, though, all the same.

And she'd taken no interest in the man, afterwards. Oh, certainly, she'd helped him to the shelter, set him up by the fire, but then, she'd curled up on the bedroll of her own, turned her back to the fire, and slept.

You are not my burden, Grayson thought, eyes flicking from the quail roasting over the fire to the man, leaning against a boulder.

There was another thought, though, that came unbidden.

But I want you to be.

The thought sparked discord in his heart—his heart that, he realized, had let go of the last love.

Let go, and he hadn't even felt it vanish.

Hadn't even known it didn't dwell in his heart anymore until it'd long since left.

In its wake, an empty sort of hurt.

"You have a name," Grayson asked dully, glancing once more to the man. He'd been quiet, without Juli, eyes glassy and unseeing.

The man glanced up, some life coming back into himself. “A name,” he echoed, voice hoarse. “I...don’t know. Do I?”

A loon.

Lilah, though, seemed unperturbed by the disorientation. “Do you remember being the bear?”

“Asking the important questions, Li,” Grayson muttered, rolling his eyes.

The man gave a quiet laugh.

Grayson glanced up.

You made him laugh.

“Remember...is the wrong word,” the man said slowly, like his tongue couldn’t quite recall how to shape the words. “Feel. I feel what it was like, in the before.” His eyes drifted to Juli. “What is she?”

“She has the Touch,” Grayson snapped.

He will never love you.

Lilah gave him a hard jab with her elbow, glaring. “Stop it,” she hissed.

“Stop what,” the man asked, watching them both.

Stop chasing after impossible loves.

That’s what she’d meant.

Stop running after people who can only break your heart.

Stop running after these monsters.

And maybe she was right.

Maybe he wasn’t that kind of boy, the kind that tamed the wild beasts.

Maybe he was something different.

He was dirt.

The best kind of dirt.

The kind that people loved for gardens, the kind where flowers flourished, the kind where plants could grow. The kind of dirt that gave and gave and gave, all summer long, and in the winter, the flora gave back, restoring him once more.

The kind of dirt that didn't deserve to be trampled on.

"Sorry," Grayson breathed, finding the man's eyes. *It's not your fault I got left with an empty place in my heart. And it isn't mine, either.*

He'd find someone.

It just wasn't this one.

Chapter 19

LILAH

LILAH FOUND HER BROTHER OUTSIDE THE SHELTER LONG AFTER night had fallen, a handful of the white pebbles in his hand.

One of three.

And so far, no sign of the ice spiders.

"You look worried," Lilah said quietly, sinking down into the snow beside Grayson. Waves of heat were rippling from her skin, a mirage dancing in the light from the fire inside, melting the ice where they sat.

"No, just..." Grayson sighed, glancing over to her. "What are we going to come home to?"

A fair question.

The months were passing them by, winter in full swing with no end in sight, and home felt years away.

"We're collecting these wards, trying to stop the Festival of Frost, and I–I want to save them," Grayson said. "But what if there's nothing to save?"

"They made their choice," Lilah shrugged. "As did we."

"You think the *vora* warned them all."

"You do, too," Lilah countered. He'd said as much, when he'd talked about Nik leaving.

He hadn't talked about Nik in a while, now.

Lilah crossed her legs, mulling it all over. Their father hadn't listened to the *vora's* warning. So, Reed had taken to the people. Told each of them, in turn, of what might be coming. Some had returned to the Capital, or else, tried to find a different settlement to take them in. Others brushed it off, as superstition, as she had. Some were afraid, and others, hopeful that perhaps this meant magic was still alive, terrible or not.

In the world below, it'd been dying.

The magic.

She felt it, in her blood, climbing up away from it all.

It withered, in the disuse. And their people were happy to let it die.

There'd been the wars.

Terrible, bloody wars, and it was better, their predecessors saw, to let the magic die than sacrifice those who carried it.

Nurtured it.

Loved it.

"When we go home," Lilah said softly, "I don't want the magic to die. I don't want to forget this fire in my blood. I don't want to relinquish any part of myself, climbing down this mountain, and I'm terrified that I will. That we'll find this ward, and as this twisted magic fades, we will, too. And we'll forget."

"Then remember," Grayson said simply.

Perhaps he had a point.

She would burn. Burn, unceasingly, unendingly, burn until all that remains is the charred earth, fertile, ready to begin again. And what was left when she was done burning, naught but the gods would imagine.

Even now, she could feel the fire sparking in defiance beneath her palms.

She would not forget.

Chapter 20

JULI

JULI FELT HIM, LAYING DOWN BESIDE HER.

The bear man.

Whatever had happened in the snow as he'd shed his fur, it had bonded them.

Bonded irreparably.

His skin was soft, his naked body warm against hers, cloaks and blankets piled around them, soaking up the heat from the fire.

Words felt...superfluous.

She said them anyway.

"Gray asked if you had a name," Juli said quietly, letting their legs tangle together.

"I wish to be called Espen," he said, after a moment of thought. "That is what I was called. Before."

"Espen," she echoed.

His hand drifted down her waist, tracing the curves of her growing belly. "You are with child," he breathed. "I can smell it on you. The scent of life. And yet you are alone."

"Not alone," she amended.

Fin was no bear in the Wilderness.

Finley, she realized, had been more lost than anyone she'd found in these woods.

"What will you do now," Juli asked quietly, watching Espen's dark eyes on her.

He shrugged. "I don't know. Part of me wishes to become the bear once more. And yet, to shed this skin, to run into the forest—that is to leave you behind, Juli with the Touch."

"There is no reason you cannot do both. Shed your skin and run wild amongst the trees. And when you wish to return home, I will sing you back to human," she smiled softly, "and we will have each other."

What a marvelous thought it was, too.

That they would have their freedom.

That their lives, so intertwined, even from the start, could diverge, only to meet again when they both grew tired.

Morning found them, quiet and still, and it was with reluctance that Juli pulled herself from Espen's arms and the cloaks atop to face the day.

The divergence.

The first, she knew, of many.

"I know the berries you're searching for," Espen explained, answering the questions over a breakfast of cold fowl. "They're atop the mountain, as the *vora* has said. You're close, though—a day's hike, perhaps less, if you move quickly."

Juli's hand drifted down, feeling the bulge across her stomach.

And how long to get home again?

The berries might be a day away.

And the leaves of green...

Maybe they were close.

And maybe it would be many months more, fending off ice spiders and men of stone and great beasts that reared their heads in the forest before they found the foliage.

She said a quiet goodbye to Espen beyond the now shattered shelter, Grayson happily dismantling his handiwork from the day before.

"Find me," she said quietly, squeezing Espen's hand.

"I could say the same to you," Espen smiled back.

"Then we will find each other," Juli nodded, determined. "Be well, Espen. Be safe."

"And you, Juli. You will sing me back to human again soon, this, I feel. You will sing me back, and then together, we will sing your child into this world. This, I promise."

With that, he took a step back, and with a roar to shake the sky above, the man was gone, a massive white bear left in his wake.

And still.

Onward.

Lilah burned the snow away, and the world with it, everything they knew disappearing beneath the plumes of white.

Juli could see why the gods had sought refuge here.

It was a view to put the heavens to shame.

As Espen said, they found the yellow berries atop the mountain, a single, scraggly bush eking out survival from the stone.

"Jules," Lilah whispered, a smile cracking across her face as she brushed a kiss against her sister's cheek, jolting into a run towards the sweet berries.

Two down, one to go.

But as Lilah reached for the berries, a shadow passed across them all, a winged screech making Lilah pause.

Her hesitation was their failing.

Without warning, a great falcon dove for the bush, snagging the last berried branch in its talons, ripping the roots from the stone as it took to the air once more.

"No!" Juli's scream echoed across the valleys, despair like she'd never known crashing down upon her.

We will sing your child into this world.

What world.

One where she'd been bested by a stupid bird?

That left her one choice.

The falcon must be felled.

She felt it, in her blood, the circle of it all. This noble creature had to fall, so that they might not.

It knew what it had done, pulling the berries from her reach.

To walk with life was to know death, and if she could sing something into the world, she could take it away, and so, the balance stayed.

A bird for a baby.

If she could bring life, then she sure as hell could take it, too.

She yanked Grayson's bow from where he'd drawn it, snapping for an arrow.

There'd been no archery lessons for young little Juli.

That hadn't stopped her as she watched from the sidelines, all the same.

Aim.

Her eyes never left the bird, swooping through the air.

Draw.

Her muscles drew from instinct, following the creature.

Loose.

With an echoing cry, the bird fell, fluttering into the valley below, but not before releasing the branch, heavy with the yellow berries.

It fell to the mountain top, scattering the fruit across the stone, and Lilah gave a shriek of triumph, almost in tears.

Juli couldn't stop herself from popping a berry into her mouth—just one.

Sweet. Juicy.

Perfect.

The taste of triumph.

Chapter 21

GRAYSON

PEBBLES.

Berries.

That left just one.

Just one.

But between them and the leaves of green, trouble.

From where the falcon had tumbled, dead into the valley, out crawled all sorts of mischief, seeking revenge.

Ice spiders and stone men, frozen rockwolves with howling calls, beast and bird and shadows, too, looking to revel in the Festival of Frost.

And so, it reached the fever-pitch.

"What do we do," Lilah breathed, watching the creatures clamoring up the mountainside.

The gods had sought refuge, here, atop the mountain.

They were not gods, though.

Sitting on the top of the world wouldn't do them much good.

The shifting earth was futile against the onslaught. Stone men were one thing–falcons and shadows were another.

"Whatever we do, we can't let them escape," Juli said quietly, watching in horror. "Whatever our world is, they are not of it. They do not belong. They are from a time where gods could sit from their mountaintops, and that era is past." Her eyes flicked to Grayson. Then to Lilah.

They knew what to do.

Rending the earth up, up, up, Grayson filled the gaps below, creatures crying in dismay.

And Lilah watched them burn.

Her fire ran down the mountainsides, an avalanche, eating everything in its path. Flames licked the birds from the sky, chased the shadows back into their caverns, sent the herds of ice spiders curling, charcoaled and black, cast the beasts into nothing but ash.

And when she had burned the foul creatures, she burned the stone.

Burned the earth.

Burned the sky.

Burned it all.

In the wake of her wrath, ash.

And it was a curious thought.

Wondering who they'd all been, before the ash.

"Li," Juli breathed, not daring to touch her sister.

Lilah crumpled, though, unhearing.

She had burned so hard, she'd burned herself out.

Juli would mend her, though.

Grayson was taken with something else.

Across the ashen countryside, green.

Leaves of green.

He recognized it, from the books of his childhood, long ago. Wakened in the heart of fire. Blossomed in the cold of winter.

First, the pebbles, white as snow, round and smooth and brought from below.

Second, the berries, yellow as day, sweet and juicy and out of the way.

Third, the leaves as green as spring, winter's bounty to me you'll bring.

And when you gather your sacrifice three, only then, they'll leave you be.

Done.

They had made it.

Made it to the end of such a terrible, horrible, wonderful, irreplaceable nightmare.

Chapter 22

LILAH

LILAH AWOKE HUDDLED BENEATH HER BLANKET, CURLED IN A TIGHT ball.

Dawn was just now peering through the window, covered in a fractal pattern of white frost crawling across the glass.

Her breath frosted the air as she pulled the blanket tighter, exhaling deeply.

Just a dream.

That's all it'd been.

The spot beside her was empty, still.

Juli hadn't come back last night to chatter on about her boys, the way she always did, bright and loquacious and singing a little bit of life into this gods-forsaken place with her sing-song voice.

Lilah missed her, she realized in the cold morning.

Missed her badly.

The breakfast bell echoed through the settlement, beckoning her below.

Lilah found the kitchen of the cabin crammed with faces she'd seen a thousand times and didn't recognize, everyone hoping to grab a bowl of hotgrain before the day began.

And her thoughts moved back to the dream.

How sweetly it had burned.

How deeply she'd been loved, in that dream. Loved by herself. Loved by her brother and sister. Loved by the magic she wished she had been born with.

But it was a dream.

A dream, and nothing more.

Even now, it was fleeting.

Slipping away as she rubbed the sleep from her eyes.

How badly, though, she wanted to remember.

"Weather's movin' in," someone grumbled.

Not like in the dream, it wasn't.

"Winter's on it's way," someone else added. "Frost like that?"

A Festival, she thought resentfully.

If it was going to be a proper festival, they'd need some decorations. A bit of holly, for one, hanging over the mantle.

Pushing back the bench, Lilah was fighting a faint tug on her lips as she left the bowl of hotgrain abandoned, turning for the door.

A bit of holly...and she knew just where to find it.

Chapter 23

JULI

IT WAS ODD, JULI THOUGHT, LOOKING AT THE FROST THAT COATED the settlement overnight.

Bile was biting at the back of her tongue.

Odder still, the dream she'd had.

The Touch.

She could recall little of what she'd dreamt, but she remembered that much.

That her hands could heal, and she'd sung life back into the world.

"If I wanted to run away," Juli asked softly, glancing over to Fin, "what would you say?"

A smile split across Fin's face as he linked arms with her. "I'd say yes. A chance to take you and get out of this gods-forsaken hell-hole? No question."

And for a moment, she could see it.

Fin, from the dream.

Someone was making a fuss, across the settlement, though, and she lost the thought, eyes drifting to the chaos.

"Who's that," Juli muttered, watching as a young man in a fur-lined cloak approached their father, his shock of white hair blazing in the sun.

"Dunno," Fin shrugged. "Some bloke. Aspen. Epsom? Anyway. What's this nonsense about running away, Jules? You serious?"

She didn't take her eyes from the stranger as she shook her head. "No. No, it...it's a sweet dream, I think, but this is my home, now." She glanced back to Fin. "He looks straight out of one of Bess's tales, doesn't he?"

Fin only scoffed, looking away. "I've been telling you, Jules. You're listening to too many stories. You oughta leave that behind. Grow up a bit."

There was nothing left to do, then.

"I think you're right," Juli mused, giving him a pat on the arm. "I'll see you later, Fin. It's been fun, but..." She jerked her head towards the man with the white hair, the man now watching her with a grin on his face. "I think I rather fancy seeing what sort of tale he's crawled out of, if you take my meaning."

She left Fin standing in the road, slack jawed, a glare blossoming on his brow.

The world was made for the living.

Perhaps it'd just been a dream.

That didn't mean, though, she couldn't sing a little bit of life back into this place, all the same.

The clouds were gathering atop the mountains.

There was a storm coming, to be sure.

"Hi, there," she grinned, meeting the man where he stood before the cabin. "You find the Basin okay?"

A bright smile was on his lips as he gave a nod. "No problem. This place..." He glanced around, eyes sparkling. "It's teeming with life."

Then, reaching into his cloak, he pulled out a little pouch, offering it out. "Name's Espen, by the way. Berry?"

Chapter 24

GRAYSON

GRAYSON AWOKE IN THE HORSE-BLANKET-AND-HAY BED, HIGH IN THE loft of the barn, the cold dawn dancing through the roof slats.

The night before came rushing back.

What a dream he had dreamed.

It felt like years, tumbling in the hay with Nik.

Nik, who was leaving, Grayson remembered, wakefulness finding him fully, now.

There was something he had to do.

"Hey!" Grayson's voice carried across the yard as he made for the blacksmith's boy, stuffing full a saddlebag.

Nik glanced up, a grin cracking across his tired face. "Long time, no—"

"Shut up," Grayson snapped, meeting him face to face. "First off, you can go straight to hell. You knew you were leaving when you dragged me up there, and I had a right to know about the lies, Nik. I had a right to know that you were just playing along for the sake of a good fuck. Second, you get the hell out of this place, and third, don't you fucking dare look back, do you hear me? You go, and you keep on going until you think you're about to drop, and then you go a little further, because I..." He trailed off, brow softening. "I loved you," Grayson murmured. "I loved you, Nik. And I deserved better than you."

Turning, he let Nik's protestations get lost in the wind, where they belonged.

Dark clouds had started moving in, now, big, heavy drops of rain starting to pelt the dirt.

Hell of a dream, that'd been.

One where he'd hurt over that boy for so many gods-damned months, it was unreal.

Grayson kicked the dirt. It'd felt so good, dreaming of moving mountains.

Dreaming of healing that wound, eventually.

In the blink of an eye, the rain had shifted, turning to hail, and Grayson swore, jogging for the barn.

That was the Basin, though. Weather was liable to shift like that.

"Hey! C'mere!"

Grayson slowed to a walk beneath the overhang of a house where the voice had beckoned him from.

"You're gonna get hurt," a young man frowned, gesturing Grayson to join him on the porch. "People don't think it's dangerous. It's like rocks, though, pelted from the sky."

"Yeah," Grayson murmured, eyes drifting to the hunks of ice accumulating in the dirt.

Something familiar...

As quickly as it'd come, though, it began to trail off, the din subsiding to a quiet roar, until it faded off completely.

And he remembered.

"That's it–hold up, you–I didn't even get your name," Grayson stumbled, torn.

"Jake."

"Jake, I–I swear, I will be right back," Grayson said, a smile tugging at his lips. "Thank you, I–just don't move a muscle, alright? I will be right back."

The man named Jake just grinned, crossing his arms. "Me? Leave? I wouldn't dare."

Epilogue

LILAH

"MARY!"

It was useless, calling out.

Juli's voice had been lost on the wind, and the little girl was long gone in a whirl of giggles.

"They don't listen," Lilah teased, leaning back in the rocking chair on the porch. Her eyes flicked to her sister, sitting on the bench with her arm around Espen. "It's in their nature."

"That much is true," Grayson put in, glancing over to Jake. "I can't get Noah to do hardly anything these days. That child will be the death of me, I swear."

Lilah hoped that wasn't true.

They'd buried their father, last year.

It was too soon for another funeral.

Ten years, and this place had started to feel like home.

They'd managed to squeeze a little magic back into the Basin, in her humble opinion.

The clouds in the distance boasted weather.

Hail, Lilah hoped.

Hail, to start the Festival of Frost.

It'd been such a stupid thing, the Festival. Three children, grasping at straws. Three children, treading water, trying to find some glimmer of hope in the dream they'd never talked about.

Sure enough, the familiar patter of ice on rooftops sent a barrage of white pebbles scattering about the settlement, that afternoon.

And so, they beckoned in the Festival.

The first storm after the frost, to welcome the changing seasons.

They'd set up the kitchen table for the decorations, Lilah and Juli and Grayson, and all the Basin kids were clamoring to help, bringing in their pails of ice marbles, plunking them into the bottom of glasses, waiting.

It'd been Juli's idea, tying ribbon around them, making them look all lovely, the sprigs of berries and holly little make-shift winter bouquets.

Each year, they took turns, telling of the dream.

Of the mountain elf that had descended to warn of the Festival.

Of the ice spiders that the fire-render chased away in the night as she'd found her flame, and her skin that burned so bright none dared touch her, lest they burn, too.

Of the pebbles the earth-mover rained down from above, and the berries at the top of the mountain, and the fever-bush that sprouted all along the hills in the wake of flame.

Of the Sleeping Stones and the shadows, of the man who shed his skin to run with the bears, and his lover who sang him back when he came home.

Of magic.

Never forgotten.

Acknowledgements

As with most major life decisions, this story came as an impulse, and so, I would like to thank the handful of people who hung on through the whirlwind of bringing it to life.

My husband, for believing in Lilah, Juli, and Grayson before I ever did.

Lauren, for showing me the world needs my voice.

Stephen, for seeing inspiration where I only saw desperation.

I'd also like to thank my family, found and otherwise, for helping keep the magic alive. When I doubted myself, you never did, and that has made a world of difference.

Of course, I'd be remiss if I didn't thank anyone who took the time to read this story. I hope that it gave you something you needed, and if it didn't, I hope that you find whatever you're looking for.

As a joke, once, I thanked myself for putting in the work, and so, with a bit more sincerity this time, I would like to do so again. It's very scary, I think, penning the story you need to hear–and need to write–but it's been an incredible process. There is a certain amount of self-acceptance required to pen reflections of yourself, self-acceptance I unequivocally needed as I continue to affirm within myself it's alright to break the mold. For everyone feeling the same, I wish you the bravery that writing helped me find.

Lastly, I'd like to thank my characters, for letting me take them on such a grand adventure.

Lilah, for showing me that independence isn't incompatible with accepting love. Juli, for showing me that life has a funny way of bringing people to you. Grayson, for showing me that we all deserve better than we think.

Thank you.

About the Author

C.H. Williams is an author, scholar, and occasional musician living in a vaguely coastal region out East. When not causing trouble or spending time with their husband, C.H. can often be found playing with their very energetic dog, scribbling away on the next new project, or zoning out to some tunes whilst enjoying nature.

THE ADVENTURE CONTINUES.

chwilliamsliterary.com

@chwilliamsliterary